D1311225

EPB KRASNER

Krasner, Steven.

The longest game

HUDSON PUBLIC LIBRARY
3 WASHINGTON ST
@WOOD SQUARE
HUDSON, MA 01749

WITHDRAWN
FROM OUR
COLLECTION

HUDSON
PUBLIC LIBRARY

HUDSON PUBLIC LIBRARY
WOOD SQUARE
HUDSON, MA 01749

FEB 0 3 2012

For my parents, Julius and Lorraine; my wife, Sue; our children, Amy, Jeffrey and Emily, and my sister, Marie. And to my brother, Mike. Thanks for all those hours of batting practice -- S.K.

For my three sons, Mark, Alex and Lincoln, with love -- S.S.

No part of this publication may be reproduced in whole or in part, or stored in a retrieval system, or transmitted in any form or by any means, electronic, mechanical, photocopying, recording, or otherwise, without written permission of the publisher, with the exception of a reviewer, who may quote brief passages in a review.
For information regarding permission, write to Gorilla Productions, 44 Bayberry Lane, East Greenwich, R.I., 02818.

Text copyright © 1996 by Steven Krasner
Illustrations copyright © 1996 by Susan Starkweather
All rights reserved. This edition published by Gorilla Productions.
Second Gorilla Productions Printing, 1997
Third Gorilla Productions Printing, 2001
Commemorative 25th Anniversary Printing, 2006
Fifth Gorilla Productions Printing, 2007
Commemorative 30th Anniversary Printing, 2011
Library of Congress Catalog Card Number 96-094053
ISBN 0-9642721-1-3

 Gorilla Productions

It was a baseball game.

One team won.

One team lost.

But it was a special baseball game, so special it was even given its own name.

The Longest Game.

In the history of professional baseball, no two teams ever played a longer game than the minor-league Pawtucket Red Sox and the Rochester Red Wings played in 1981 at McCoy Stadium in Pawtucket, R.I.

A baseball game usually lasts 9 innings. But the Pawtucket Red Sox and the Rochester Red Wings were tied after 9 innings.

So they kept playing to see which team would win. And they kept playing. And they kept playing some more.

They played 33 innings before Pawtucket won, 3-2.

The game began on a cold, windy April 18 night. It continued through the even colder and windier early morning hours of Easter Sunday, April 19. A halt was called after 32 innings, the exhausted teams tied at 2-2 and only 27 fans left in the stands.

The Longest Game was re-started and completed on a warm, festive June 23 night in front of 5,756 fans and newspaper, television and radio people from all around the country, as well as from England and Japan.

"Absolutely unbelievable," said Pawtucket manager Joe Morgan at the time.

Unbelievable, but true.

It's all there in the record books. It's all there in a display at the Baseball Hall of Fame in picturesque Cooperstown, N.Y.

JOE MORGAN

CAL RIPKEN, JR.

WADE BOGGS

RED WINGS

Many of the players in The Longest Game made it to the major leagues.

Some, like Rochester's Cal Ripken Jr. and Pawtucket's Wade Boggs, became superstars. Some, like Pawtucket's Dave Koza, who got the game-winning hit, never made it to the major leagues. Joe Morgan made it as a manager. So did Rochester manager Doc Edwards.

They all have one very special thing in common, however. They all are part of baseball history.

But they had no idea they were about to participate in anything special when they arrived at McCoy Stadium on Saturday, April 18, 1981.

They did know it was cold, though. Very cold. They knew strong winds were blowing in at the small ballpark, so strong it was impossible to hit a home run.

And they soon found out one of the light towers wasn't working, causing a half-hour delay at the start.

The game finally began at 8 o'clock. It seemed like just another game. Nothing special. Pawtucket was losing, 1-0. But the Pawsox tied the game at 1-1 in the bottom of the 9th, sending the game into extra innings.

No one was thinking about baseball history then. It was too cold. And besides, most extra-inning games are decided in a few innings or so.

Not this time, though.

The game dragged on. It was cold. And getting colder.

The players tried to keep warm as best they could. When they weren't on the field, they were in the locker room, drinking coffee and hot chocolate. They put on extra pairs of long underwear.

Some players even tossed broken bats into an empty garbage barrel and lit them on fire. They held their hands over the fire to warm their frozen fingers.

There were 1,740 fans at the game when it started. That number kept going down as the temperature went down and the innings piled up. The remaining fans huddled under blankets to keep warm.

At 1 o'clock on Easter morning, Pawtucket Red Sox officials Ben Mondor, Mike Tamburro and Lou Schwechheimer noticed an International League rule that said no inning could start after 12:50 a.m.

Unfortunately, the umpires' rule book didn't contain the same rule.

So the teams kept playing.

And playing.

Pawtucket officials tried calling Harold Cooper, the league's commissioner, for an official ruling.

He wasn't home at 1:30. He wasn't home at 2 o'clock. He wasn't home at 2:30.

So they kept playing.

And playing.

Rochester scored a run in the top of the 21st inning. Finally, it looked like the long night would come to an end.

But Pawtucket tied the score in the bottom of the 21st inning. Wade Boggs drove in the tying run.

So they kept playing.

And playing.

"I didn't know whether to boo him, kiss him or kill him," said Debbie Boggs, Wade's wife, who still was at the game with the couple's two-year-old daughter, Meagann.

Joe Morgan argued an umpire's call in the 22nd inning. He was thrown out of the game for arguing. Pitching coach Mike Roarke replaced him as manager for the rest of the game.

They kept playing.

And playing.

Pawtucket Red Sox officials finally reached Harold Cooper. He said if the game still was tied after the inning they were playing, to stop playing for the night.

Rochester had a chance to win the game in that inning, the 32nd. But Pawtucket outfielder Sam Bowen threw out a runner at the plate. So the teams were tied, 2-2, after 32 innings.

They stopped playing at exactly 4:07 Easter Sunday morning. By the time the players left the field, the sun was rising.

"I feel like Jello," said Boggs.

"I wonder if the Easter Bunny is going to come hopping over the fence," said Anne Koza, Dave's wife, who sat through all 32 innings.

An exhausted Ben Mondor, the team's owner, and Tamburro, the team's general manager, closed up shop. To them, it wasn't The Longest Game. Not yet, anyway. They were too tired to think about baseball history.

To them, at that moment, it was 'That stupid darn thing."

That's how they felt after 8 hours and 7 minutes of baseball the teams suffered through April 18-19.

But "that stupid darn thing" put Pawtucket, R.I., on the map. Calls poured in from all around the country on Easter Sunday morning as the Pawtucket Red Sox and the Rochester Red Wings prepared to play that afternoon's scheduled game.

Everyone wanted to know if it was true that the teams had played 32 innings the night before.

It was true.

And the fact that they all had participated in something special began to sink in.

"The next morning, we started thinking about history," said Rochester's Dallas Williams. "Man, we just played 32 innings of baseball. We joked about it. We had smiles on our faces. I was thankful I was a baseball player and on the field that night."

But the game wasn't over.

It was still tied, 2-2.

The league, though, decided that because the players were so exhausted, they wouldn't finish the game until June 23, the next time the Red Wings visited McCoy Stadium to play Pawtucket.

And on June 23, all eyes of the baseball world were on McCoy Stadium.

Major league baseball players were on strike, so minor league baseball enjoyed the sport's spotlight. It was shining brightly on the Pawtucket Red Sox and the Rochester Red Wings.

And ultimately, the glare fell squarely on Dave Koza.

The Red Wings did not score in the top of the 33rd inning.

In Pawtucket's half of the inning, Rochester pitcher Steve Grilli hit Marty Barrett with a pitch, gave up a double to Chico Walker and intentionally walked Russ Laribee.

The bases were loaded. There were no outs. And up stepped Dave Koza to face relief pitcher Cliff Speck.

On Speck's fifth pitch, Koza hit a single to left field. Barrett gleefully jumped on home plate, and then he and Koza were mobbed on the field by their teammates, laughing and whooping and hollering and patting each other on the back.

After an exhausting 8 hours and 7 minutes of baseball on April 18-19; after another 18 minutes on June 23; after a total of 33 innings, the game finally was over.

In the Pawtucket locker room, winning pitcher Bob Ojeda and hitting hero Dave Koza were surrounded by television cameras, tape recorders and reporters with note pads. They even did interviews with Japanese writers, using translators.

Everyone wanted to know all about this one game. This one very special game.

The Longest Game.

"When we walked off the field at 4 o'clock in the morning, it was like, 'You mean we're not done with this game yet?'"

--Pawtucket catcher Rich Gedman

"I wanted 40 innings so nobody could ever tie our beautiful record."

--Pawtucket manager Joe Morgan

"I remember striking out Cal Ripken on a 3-and-2 breaking ball at 4 o'clock in the morning, and I don't think he ever forgave me."

--Pawtucket's Bruce Hurst, who pitched the 27th-32nd innings

"I've been watching for the bunt for 23 innings now."

--Rochester third baseman Cal Ripken Jr., wearily replying to relief pitcher Jim Umbarger's instruction

"Nothing I ever do in life will probably compare with this."

--Pawtucket's Dave Koza, after his historic winning hit

"A lot of people were saying, 'Yeah, yeah, we tied it, we tied it!' And then they said, 'Oh, no, what did you do? We could have gone home!'"

--Pawtucket's Wade Boggs on his game-tying hit in the 21st inning

"It sank in the next day. Man, we just played 32 innings of baseball. We joked about it. We had smiles on our faces. I was thankful I was a baseball player and on the field that night. As time went by, I appreciated it more."

--Rochester's Dallas Williams

OFFICIAL BOX SCORE

ROCHESTER	ab	r	h	bi		PAWTUCKET	ab	r	h	bi
Eaton 2b	10	0	3	0		Graham cf	14	0	1	0
Williams cf	13	0	0	0		Barrett 2b	12	1	2	0
Ripken 3b	13	0	2	0		Walker lf	14	1	2	0
Corey dh	5	1	1	0		Laribee dh	11	0	0	1
Chism ph	1	0	0	0		Koza 1b	14	1	5	1
Rayford c	5	0	0	0		Boggs 3b	12	0	4	1
Logan 1b	12	0	4	0		Bowen rf	12	0	2	0
Valle 1b	1	0	0	0		Gedman c	3	0	1	0
Bourjos lf	4	0	2	1		Ongarato ph	1	0	0	0
Hale lf	7	0	1	0		LaFrancois c	8	0	2	0
Smith lf	0	0	0	0		Valdez ss	13	0	2	0
Hazewood rf	4	0	0	0						
Hart rf	6	1	1	0						
Bonner ss	12	0	3	0						
Huppert c	11	0	1	1						
Putnam ph	1	0	0	0						
Totals	**105**	**2**	**18**	**2**		**Totals**	**114**	**3**	**21**	**3**

No outs when winning run scored.

E – Eaton, Logan, Bonner, Valdez. DP – Rochester 4. Pawtucket 3, LOB – Rochester 30, Pawtucket 23. 2B – Koza 2, Walker, Boggs, Huppert. SB – Eaton. S – Williams 2, Logan, Hart, Huppert 2. SF – Laribee.

ROCHESTER	IP	H	R	ER	BB	SO
Jones	8⅔	7	1	1	2	5
Schneider	5⅓	2	0	0	0	8
Luebber	8	6	1	1	2	4
Umbarger	10	4	0	0	0	9
Grilli (L)	0	1	1	1	1	0
Speck	0	1	0	0	0	0

PAWTUCKET	IP	H	R	ER	BB	SO
Parks	6	3	1	1	4	3
Aponte	4	0	0	0	2	9
Sarmiento	4	3	0	0	2	3
Smithson	3⅔	2	0	0	3	5
Remmerswaal	4⅓	4	1	1	3	3
Finch	5	3	0	0	1	3
Hurst	5	2	0	0	3	7
Ojeda (W)	1	1	0	0	0	1

Parks pitched to 3 batters in the 7th; Grilli pitched to 3 batters in the 33rd; Speck pitched to 1 batter in the 33rd.
WP – Jones, Smithson, Hurst, HPB – by Schneider (Laribee), by Parks (Eaton), by Aponte (Bonner), by Grilli (Barrett).
T – 8:25. A – 1,740.